SOCCER STEP-UP

BY JAKE MADDOX
text by
Eric Stevens

STONE ARCH BOOKS
a capstone imprint

Jake Maddox JV Girls books are published by
Stone Arch Books
a Capstone imprint
1710 Roe Crest Drive
North Mankato, Minnesota 56003

www.mycapstone.com

Library of Congress Cataloging-in-Publication Data is available on the Library of Congress website.

ISBN: 978-1-4965-3675-4 (library binding)
ISBN: 978-1-4965-3679-2 (paperback)
ISBN: 978-1-4965-3683-9 (ebook PDF)

Summary: The middle school soccer program has been cut, and now eighth grader Melina Stern and her teammates are trying out for the high school JV team. But it's soon clear that the older players don't want the middle schoolers around, and the girls are having trouble playing as a team.

Art Director: Nathan Gassman
Designer: Kayla Rossow
Media Researcher: Morgan Walters
Production Specialist: Tori Abraham

Photo Credits:
Shutterstock: Aaron Amat, (basketball) 96, Amy Myers, Cover, Angie Makes, design element, Bplanet, design element, cluckva, design element, Dan Kosmayer, (stick) 96, Eky Studio, design element, irin-k, (soccer ball) 96, Lightspring, (volleyball) 96

Printed in the United States of America in Stevens Point, Wisconsin.
009622F16

TABLE OF CONTENTS

CHAPTER 1

RIVALS

Where are you, Ms. Perez? Melina Stern wondered as she gripped the chain-link fence around the athletic field and stretched her quadriceps. She let out a frustrated sigh.

Today was the Delano Middle School soccer team's first day of practice. All the girls had been busy stretching and warming up for the past fifteen minutes. But the coach, Ms. Perez, was a no-show.

Nora Kahn came up to Melina and jogged in place. "Maybe you should just go home," she said.

She flashed a sly grin, like a big bad wolf. "I can lead practice today."

Melina and Nora had been playing on school teams, at soccer camps, and in after-school intensives together since they were four. They were teammates, but they had also become something else — rivals.

"You're hilarious," Melina said, reaching for her toes to stretch her hamstrings and calves. "I can wait just as long as you can."

The other girls were warming up too, but they kept an eye on the two strikers. Now that Nora and Melina were in eighth grade, the team expected their best players to lead them.

"I have an idea," Melina said, straightening up. She called out to the group, "Why don't we do the captain vote? Get it out of the way while we wait."

For an instant, Melina saw Nora frown in fear, clearly caught off guard. If Melina didn't know her so well, she might have missed it. Then it was gone, and the sinister grin was back.

"Sounds like a plan," Nora agreed. She turned to the team. "I nominate Melina Stern."

Melina shot her rival a look. "And I nominate Nora Kahn," she replied.

Nora smiled big. "Thanks. Any other nominees?"

When no one said anything, Nora continued. "Vote by a show of hands? Sound good?"

Melina noticed some of the girls shuffling uncomfortably, but no one spoke up. That seemed good enough for Nora.

"Great," Nora said, clapping her hands together. "Raise your hands to vote for, um . . . me!"

Five or six girls raised their hands. Melina thought seventh grader Ginger Adams was only doing it because Nora was watching.

But the small number of hands gave Melina a huge confidence boost. She stepped forward. "And who votes for me?" she asked.

The rest of the hands went up. Melina grinned. "Looks like a landslide," she whispered to Nora.

For the first time Melina could remember, Nora couldn't muster a smile at all.

"Ladies, ladies," called a familiar voice. Melina looked up and saw Ms. Perez, eighth-grade history teacher and soccer coach, striding onto the athletic field. "So sorry I'm late."

Melina waved and ran to greet her. As she went, she noticed the coach was still in her teaching clothes — black pants and a white blouse, even her sensible black shoes. And she wasn't carrying a big mesh bag of soccer balls, either.

That's weird, Melina thought. *What's going on?*

"Hi, Melina!" Ms. Perez said, giving Melina a hug when she reached her. "Sorry I was so late."

"Hi, Coach! That's all right," Melina replied. She started walking with Ms. Perez back toward the team. "We've just been warming up."

Ms. Perez sighed and stopped at the edge of the field. "I wish I'd been as productive this afternoon as you girls have been."

"What happened?" Melina asked.

"I've been on the phone since the last bell rang," Ms. Perez explained. She shook her head. "But some things can't be fixed."

Melina frowned. Her coach was obviously upset. "Maybe this will cheer you up," she offered. "We did the captain vote while we waited — I won!"

"Oh, Melina," Ms. Perez said, giving her shoulders a squeeze. "You deserve it."

"Thanks," Melina said, beaming proudly.

"But I'm sorry to say . . . you won't get to be captain," the coach went on.

Melina's heart seemed to sink into her stomach. "What? Why not?" she asked. "We voted fair and square. Even Nora's okay with the team's choice."

"That's just the thing," Ms. Perez said, looking out over the crew of soccer players. "The team doesn't get a choice, because this year there isn't going to be any team at all."

CHAPTER 2

ANOTHER WAY

"I don't get it, Ms. Perez," Nora said. She and the rest of the girls stood in a half circle around Ms. Perez and Melina. They had all just been told the terrible news. "How could this happen?"

For once, Melina agreed with her rival. Soccer was her life. What would she do without her team?

Ms. Perez offered a half shrug. "Well, the city schools have had to make lots of cuts due to budget constraints — there also won't be boys' middle school soccer or boys' swim and dive this year."

"What are budget constraints?" called out Holly Bing from the back.

"That means they're outta money," Nora answered with a smirk.

Ms. Perez nodded. "That's the general idea," she admitted.

"So we won't be able to play any soccer at *all*?" asked one of the sixth grade girls.

"Yeah," said the girl sitting behind her. "Because my parents said they can't afford to put me on one of the club teams this year."

Melina glanced at the worried sixth grade players. She had seen both of them around, but she didn't know their names. Without a soccer team, she probably wouldn't ever learn their names, either.

"Well, of course you girls can always get together to play soccer, if you make the time,"

Ms. Perez said. "But I'm afraid I don't have any other options for you sixth graders."

Melina looked up at her hopefully. "What about for the eighth graders?" she asked.

"And seventh graders?" asked Prissy Wilkins. She had been on the team with Melina last year.

"There I do have some good news," Ms. Perez said, "depending on how you look at it."

"What do you mean?" Melina asked.

"I wasn't just on the phone with the money people this afternoon," Ms. Perez explained. "I've also been talking with the junior varsity coach at the high school, Coach Naranjo."

Melina felt a flutter of excitement, despite the sad situation. Ms. Perez was talking about Coach *Maya* Naranjo, former captain of the Bulloch High School varsity team. When Melina was seven, she had seen Maya play. She had been amazing. Melina had dreamed of playing on the high school team ever since.

"I made a suggestion, and I got the school board's approval," Ms. Perez continued as a smile began to form on her lips. "Coach Naranjo was okay with the idea too, so we're going to give it a shot."

"Tell us already!" Nora said, bouncing on her toes.

"Yeah, Ms. Perez," Melina said quietly. She had an idea what her coach was going to say, but it was too wonderful to believe. "What's the plan?"

"All seventh and eighth graders are invited to try out for the high school's junior varsity team," Ms. Perez said, and her lips bloomed into a hundred-watt smile.

Melina smiled too. She had a chance to play soccer after all! *And not just any soccer,* she reminded herself. *But high school soccer, coached by former all-star striker Maya Naranjo!*

"Wait, what?" Nora said. She was *not* smiling. "We're supposed to try out against high school girls? They'll clobber us!" A few of the girls nodded in agreement.

"The JV team is mostly ninth and tenth graders," Melina pointed out. "The really strong players will be on the varsity team."

Ms. Perez nodded. "I think you're right about that," she said. "Still, you'll all have to show Coach Naranjo your best if you want a chance to play on a school team this year."

Suddenly, Melina realized something else. "Wait, what about you, Ms. Perez?"

"I'll be the JV team's assistant coach," the coach replied. "So I'll be around plenty, don't worry about that."

Melina nodded, relieved that not everything was changing. She was still disappointed that there wasn't a middle school team and that she wouldn't be their captain. But the idea of playing on a high school team was thrilling. Melina was ready to up her game.

"Okay," Nora said, pacing back and forth. "So when do we try out? How much practice time do I have?"

She seems nervous, Melina noticed. *Nora's usually super confident — over confident, even. Where did it all go?*

"You have two days," Ms. Perez said. "Tryouts are tomorrow at three thirty, right here." She pointed firmly at the ground they were standing on: the shared athletic field between the middle school and high school.

"We won't let you down," Melina assured her.

"Of course you won't," Ms. Perez said. "But just to be sure, let's practice."

Melina gave her a puzzled look. "Practice? But you're not in your sweats, and we don't have any soccer balls."

"I was in a hurry," Ms. Perez said. She pulled a lanyard from her pocket and handed it to Melina. The key to the equipment room dangled from the strap. "We still have an hour or so. Might as well make the most of it." She turned to the group and added, "Prissy, help her out, please."

Together the two girls hurried to the equipment room.

"Think we have a chance of making the high school team?" Prissy asked.

"It'll be tough," Melina said, "but I think we might!"

The truth was, though, Melina was confident that by this time next week, she'd be on the junior varsity team.

CHAPTER 3

TRYOUTS

School on Thursday was a muddled blur. All Melina could think about were the JV tryouts. But she was more excited than nervous — this was her chance to play soccer on a more advanced level.

She looked around at the other middle school girls waiting for tryouts to start. There were nine of them, gathered on the shared athletic field between the middle school and high school. They wore their gold and maroon sweats, and many were nervously bouncing up and down.

Twenty yards away, the high school JV hopefuls had gathered as well. They were wearing the blue and white colors of Bulloch High School. A couple of them were juggling soccer balls with their knees and feet and heads.

"Look at them," Nora whispered beside her. "Practically pros. I bet you can't do that."

"Maybe *you* can't. But I totally could, no problem," Melina shot back. She wasn't about to let Nora psych her out today.

"So, you nervous?" Nora asked.

Melina let out a soft snort. "Of course not," she said. "Are *you*?"

"Nope, not at all," replied Nora quietly, shoving her hands into the pockets of her hoodie. She caught Melina's eye and gave a small smile.

FWEET! FWEET! Two sharp whistles broke the chilly air. All the girls looked up to find Coaches Naranjo and Perez striding onto the athletic field.

"Good afternoon, girls," Coach Naranjo called.

She was a foot shorter than Ms. Perez, but far more intimidating. "If the middle schoolers could join the rest of the hopefuls, I'd appreciate it."

Melina and her old teammates jogged over to the high schoolers. The older girls glared at them.

"Wow, I'm feeling so welcome," Prissy whispered.

Melina frowned. She hated to admit it, but joining the high school girls on JV was starting to seem a little less than perfect. They didn't look like they wanted any middle schoolers on their team.

Coach Naranjo stood in front of the soccer players. "So it's kind of a weird year," she said. "For those who haven't figured it out, we've invited girls from the middle school to try out for JV."

"Do we get extra credit for *babysitting*?" cracked one of the high school girls. A few players laughed.

Melina recognized the girl as Laney Mendez. She'd been on the middle school team when Melina was in sixth grade and had been really nice. *But looks like things have changed,* Melina thought.

Coach Naranjo clapped her hands to quiet the crew. "All right, all right. Now that we've all gotten that out of our systems, let's get down to tryouts."

"Right," Ms. Perez agreed. "First up, five laps around the field."

Melina blew out a big breath as she hustled to the sidelines and tried to avoid getting in the way of any of the older girls. JV tryouts had officially started.

* * *

After forty-five minutes of intense practice, Melina thought she couldn't last another second. Then Coach Naranjo called the players together.

"We've got about fifteen minutes left," she said. "I want everyone to line up side by side."

The players followed the coach's instructions. The high schoolers stood on one end and the middle school girls clumped together at the other.

"As I go down the line, count off every other," Coach Naranjo said. "One, two, one, two . . ."

Like that, the girls numbered off until everyone was either on team one or team two. Melina was on two. Prissy and Holly on either side of her ended up on team one.

"Those are our scrimmage teams," Coach Naranjo said. "Team two, grab some jerseys from the box, please."

Melina hustled to grab her bright scrimmage jersey — she never knew when the coaches were watching — and knocked into Nora. "Oh, sorry."

"No worries," Nora replied, grinning. "So, looks like we're on the same team, huh?"

Melina pulled on her jersey. "Obviously."

"Well, try not to get in my way," Nora said. "I'm about to show the coaches my awesome skills."

Melina rolled her eyes and started to shoot back a reply. But before she could say anything, Nora had jogged off.

Huffing out a frustrated sigh, Melina joined the others on the sideline. Coach Naranjo was already calling girls from each team onto the field.

After a few minutes, Melina was brought into the scrimmage. *Now's my chance to show Coach Naranjo my skills,* she thought.

Before long, she had gotten the ball. She started dribbling it hard up the field. As she reached the defense, Melina caught sight of the coaches on the sidelines watching her. She decided to give them a show while she threw off her defender.

Melina darted to the right, stopped the ball against her ankle for an instant, and kicked it up. She chest-bumped the ball, and as soon it landed at her feet, she charged toward the goal.

But it didn't work. The defender had barely lost her footing during Melina's move. Now Melina found herself up against two defenders at the top of the penalty arc.

"Nice move, show-off," said one of the girls as she raced forward. She shoved her shoulder into Melina as the two struggled for the ball. "Too bad it didn't work."

Melina's heart thumped loudly as she fought to keep control of the ball. Out of the corner of her eye, she spotted Nora racing down the side. She didn't want to give her rival a chance at goal, but there was no other way to shake her opponents.

Gulping down her nerves, Melina got a foot on the ball and then spun left. The defenders stumbled after Melina as she passed to Nora.

Nora easily received the ball, barely breaking her stride. Just before entering the penalty box, she fired a shot at the net.

The goalkeeper dove across the goal and caught the ball. She punted it back up field.

No goal, but it was a good play, Melina told herself. She glanced at the sidelines just in time to see Coach Naranjo scribbling on her clipboard.

After two more plays and a close shot on goal, Melina trotted off the field as another middle school player took her place. She took a gulp from her water bottle and watched as the clock ticked down.

Soon the fifteen minutes were up. Team one had the lead, 1–0.

"Gather round, ladies!" Coach Naranjo shouted.

The exhausted players grouped up in front of the coaches, although the high schoolers still stood off to the side. Melina caught an occasional scowl from the older girls, but she just tried to focus on the coach's final announcements.

"I'll post the new team roster tomorrow morning outside my office at Bulloch High," Coach Naranjo said. "Ms. Perez will also hang the list in the middle school. Dismissed!"

With that, tryouts were over. The coaches stayed to go over their notes and make the final JV roster. But the girls in blue jogged to the Bulloch

High School locker room while Melina and the girls in maroon went back to the middle school.

"Yikes!" Prissy exclaimed as they left the field. "That was rough."

"Yeah," Ginger agreed. "And it wasn't just because of all those insane drills and sprints. Those high school girls were not friendly!"

Melina hung at the back of the group, listening to the girls' chatter. She didn't feel like talking; too many thoughts were racing through her head.

She felt confident about her performance at tryouts. She could picture herself on the JV team, wearing the Bulls blue and white.

Then Melina thought about the high schoolers' glares and their rude comments. The tiniest pinprick of fear pierced her heart. If she did make JV, those girls would be her new teammates.

Can I handle that? she wondered. *Can I play my best with teammates who don't seem to want me at all?*

CHAPTER 4

ON THE TEAM

On Friday morning, Melina was late for homeroom. So were Prissy, Holly, Ginger, Nora, and the other girls who had tried out for the team. That was because they had all stopped to check the bulletin board outside the athletics department office for the JV roster.

They had also been late for first hour and second hour. Melina and the girls now gathered around the bulletin board for the fourth time that day. If Ms. Perez didn't show up with the roster soon, they'd be late for lunch too.

"Where *is* she?" Holly said, checking the time on her phone.

Just then, Ms. Perez's confident footsteps echoed through the back hallway. "Sorry, girls," she said as she strode up to the bulletin board. "I seem to be late a lot lately, huh?"

"No big deal, Ms. Perez," Nora said. "But you do have the roster now, right?"

The coach reached into her bag and pulled out a single sheet of paper. "Right here," she said.

Ms. Perez slid the Plexiglas cover of the athletic department's bulletin board open and pinned up the roster. In an instant, Melina and Nora were standing shoulder to shoulder, gazing up at the list.

Nora's eyes were fastest. "Kahn!" she shouted, jumping up and down. "I made it!"

Melina's eyes glided past Nora's name. She kept scanning to the bottom of the list.

"Stern!" she said. Her heart fluttered with excitement. "I made it. And you too, Prissy."

"Yes!" Prissy hissed behind her.

"Wait, what about me?" Holly called from behind. She shoved her way closer to the board.

"And me!" said Ginger.

Ms. Perez shook her head. "Sorry, girls. We had to make some tough choices. Although I want you to know I fought for each and every one of you."

Ginger's shoulders sagged, but Holly shrugged. "It's no big deal," she said. "I'm actually kind of relieved. I mean, just the tryouts were too stressful. I lost two nights of sleep, and I've got a crick in my neck."

"Is that where that came from?" Nora said. She pressed her hand to the back of her neck. "I wondered why it hurt this morning."

Melina faked a chuckle. But her stomach was twisting in knots. Holly's confession about her nerves was enough to bring Melina's own doubts back to the front of her mind. *Am I really ready to play with the high schoolers?* she wondered.

"Um, I better go," she told the girls. "I'm off to the library — I have a lot of homework to catch up on. You guys can head to lunch without me."

The truth was, though, Melina was much too nervous to eat.

* * *

The first Bulloch High JV soccer practice was the next Monday. Melina and Prissy walked together across the shared athletic field toward the high school. They had both been in the high school gym plenty of times — to cheer on the basketball team and for fundraisers. But today they were heading for the locker room. That would be a first.

"You ready for this, Mel?" Prissy asked.

Melina looked at her friend. Prissy looked so sure of herself. Melina's stomach was still tangled up with nerves.

"I think so," Melina replied. *Maybe?* she added silently.

Prissy pulled the gym doors open. "I'm sure it'll be fine," she said. "I mean, we made the team. Those high schoolers will know we're not babies."

"Yeah, we've proved ourselves. They'll definitely welcome us onto the team now," Melina added sarcastically.

Prissy chuckled. "No doubt."

The girls' footsteps echoed through the empty gym as they crossed over to the locker room. With a deep breath, Melina pushed the door and went in.

As soon as they stepped into the humid warmth of the locker room, Melina saw a group of high schoolers gathered in the second row. They were standing around a girl who was sitting on the wooden bench — a girl with a wicked smile.

"Oh no," Melina whispered, grabbing Prissy's hand. "Nora got here first."

"Oh! Hey, guys," Nora said when she spotted Melina and Prissy.

The gang of ninth and tenth graders turned around. Everyone frowned at Melina, arms crossed tight across their chests.

"Mel," Nora continued, "I was just telling the team about you."

"What did you say?" Melina asked, looking quickly from one high school girl to the next.

"Oh, nothing bad!" Nora said, leaping up from the bench. "I was just saying how you've been the best striker on every team you've ever been on. And that basically the whole team elected you as team captain. Well, when we had a team."

"Right, obviously," Melina replied. She glared at Nora, who just gave a sly smile, then slid off to the next row of lockers.

"*I* am the captain of this team," said one of the high school girls. She was tall and had a nose that looked like it had been broken a half dozen times. "Is that going to be all right with you?"

Another high school girl came up behind the captain. "Because Coach Naranjo asked us to be extra careful around you middle schoolers," she added.

"We don't want any hurt feelings," said the captain.

"It's fine," Melina said, dropping her gaze to the floor.

"Oh, well, *thank you,*" said the captain, her voice thick with sarcasm. The other ninth and tenth graders laughed as they left the locker room with her.

"Rude," Prissy muttered.

Melina bit her lip while she found her locker: number 79C in the next row. She pulled it open, and inside was a white paper sack with STERN written on the side. Her jersey.

She pulled out her new blue and white Bulloch Bulls uniform. Melina's stomach twisted again, but she slipped the jersey on.

Ready or not, it was time to join her new team out on the field.

CHAPTER 5

A NOT-SO-WARM WELCOME

Coach Naranjo started practice with stretching and jogging. A fall chill hung over the field. But by the time the coach blew three sharp whistles, Melina was sweating.

"Ladies," the coach said when the team had gathered around her.

"And girls," added one of the high schoolers. "We don't want the kids from Delano to feel left out." That got a few laughs from the other ninth and tenth grade players.

Coach Naranjo didn't say anything. She just put up a hand, and the laughter died down. Ms. Perez stood silently next to the coach.

"I wish Ms. Perez would stand up for us," Prissy whispered to Melina.

Melina nodded, but the captain — her name was Rose Torrence, Melina had learned during their warm-up laps — turned around and glared at them. "Zip it, or I'll have you two running extra laps," she snapped. "Got it?"

Melina looked at the ground. Even Prissy shifted uncomfortably under Rose's fierce gaze.

"That's what I thought," the captain muttered.

"First up, Ms. Perez will lead a ball control drill at the far end of the pitch," Coach Naranjo went on. "I'll be calling you over in pairs to the other end for some quick one-on-ones to assign positions."

Melina caught her breath. Today she'd find out if the coaches would make her a forward. It was the position she'd played every year, even when she had been second string in sixth grade.

"Let's go, girls," Coach Naranjo said. "Torrence and Menendez, stay down here for the first one-on-one."

The two tenth grade girls grinned at each other and high-fived. Melina jogged with the rest of the team to the other end of the field. Ms. Perez was already there setting up cones and a practice goal on one of the sidelines.

"Melina, Nora," Ms. Perez said as the group reached her. "Help me out. Take that stack of green cones and set them up for the Double Weave drill."

"Um . . . " Melina said, looking blankly at the cones. She felt the stares of the high school girls on her, and it made her nervous. Everything she knew about soccer drills seemed to fly from her brain.

Nora grabbed the stack of green cones and gave Melina a little elbow in the side. "Come on," she whispered. "Just like last year. You awake?"

She passed half the stack to Melina and jogged toward the opposite sideline.

As soon as Nora dropped the first cone, Melina saw what she was doing. It was a drill they had run last year. Melina had done it a hundred times.

I'm letting my nerves get to me, Melina thought as she set up the cones. *I just need to calm down and focus.*

It only took a few moments. When they had finished, Nora smiled brightly. "See?" she said. "We got this."

Melina forced a smile. But while Ms. Perez was explaining the drill, Melina couldn't help feeling the eyes of every ninth and tenth grader on her. It made her more anxious.

The girls lined up on opposite sidelines. One group stood in front of the orange cones and one in front of the green cones. Ms. Perez tapped a ball to the first girl, and she dribbled in between the green cones. When she was done, she passed the ball to the girl at the front of the other line.

Now the second girl took the ball and weaved through the orange cones. But instead of passing when she got to the end of the cones, she shot into the practice goal. After taking their turn, the players jogged to the back of the other line.

Melina was fifth in line to shoot on the practice goal. The line was moving pretty quickly, but Melina let her eyes wander to the other end of the field — over to Coach Naranjo and the captain's one-on-one match.

Rose was a strong ball handler, but so was the other girl. They were obviously great friends, though. They were showing off and laughing together even as they competed for goals and for Coach Naranjo's attention.

Melina couldn't help envying how confident they looked and how the coach laughed along with them.

"Nice shot, Torrence! Great moves, Menendez!" called Coach Naranjo.

"Wake up, Stern!" Ms. Perez shouted.

Melina pulled her eyes away from the game and realized it was her turn to run the drill. Nora was standing behind her. She had stopped the soccer ball under one foot.

"Good thing I was awake," Nora said, tapping the ball to Melina. "Or the pass would have rolled right off the field."

"Sorry," Melina said quietly. Then she added louder for everyone to hear, "Sorry."

Melina started dribbling forward, darting through the cones. *You can do this,* she thought. She kept her eye on the ball, the cones, and the goal up ahead. As she drove through the last orange cone, she drew her right leg back and slammed her laces into the ball.

It was a bad shot. The ball hit the post and bounced off toward the other sideline. The girl coming off that line had to run to retrieve it.

"Focus, Stern!" Ms. Perez called. "Hustle to the other line, and stay awake, please."

"I will," Melina mumbled as she jogged across the field.

She got into the back of the other line just as Nora took a pass and started the weave. Nora's footwork was looking good as she lightly tapped the ball through. She had obviously been staying in shape during the off-season.

Nora came out of the cones in perfect control of the ball. She shot, and it sailed beautifully into the top left corner of the goal.

"Good shot, Kahn!" Ms. Perez said.

Melina watched as a high schooler close to the front of the line nudged her friend. "Well," the girl said, "at least *one* of the middle schoolers can actually shoot."

Melina pulled in her bottom lip and bit it. It was all she could do not to cry.

CHAPTER 6

ONE-ON-ONE

"Kahn and Stern!" Ms. Perez called when practice was almost over. "You're up. One-on-one with Coach Naranjo."

"Finally," Nora said as she walked up to Melina. "We're last, you know."

"I noticed," Melina said. She just wanted the day to be done.

Together they jogged down the field toward the head coach. She stood at the far goal, a ball under one arm. "Let's hustle, girls!" Coach called.

Melina picked up her pace a bit, but Nora picked it up a bit more. Before long, they were racing. Each girl sprinted down the field as fast as she could.

"Go, Kahn!" someone called from behind them.

Melina's heart sunk. Out of the corner of her eye, she spied Nora's big grin.

It was no use. Nora beat her in their sprint to Coach Naranjo. *Just like she'll probably beat me out for the center forward position,* thought Melina bitterly.

"That's more like it," Coach Naranjo said. "This will be a good old one-on-one match, so there's no goalkeeping." She nodded toward the small practice goals set up on opposite sidelines.

Nora winked at Melina. "Good luck."

"You too," Melina mumbled.

"You can start," Coach Naranjo said to Nora, "since you won the impromptu race down the field."

Nora's smile widened. It was growing more wicked by the moment.

"And I hope you two don't mind an audience," Coach said as she placed the ball in the center of the little one-on-one field. "It looks like the rest of the team has finished up early and wants to watch."

"Great!" Nora said as the other players walked over from the Double Weave drill and surrounded the half of the pitch.

"Yeah," Melina said with a sigh. "Great."

FWEET! Coach Naranjo's whistle pierced the air. Melina's one-on-one with Nora had begun.

Nora toed the ball backward. She faked to the right and then darted left.

Melina rushed toward Nora to try to steal the ball. But her opponent kicked it between her feet. Nora slid around Melina to charge the goal.

Sprinting after her, Melina moved in front of the small practice net just as Nora took the shot.

Melina reached out her leg. The ball hit the toe of her cleat and flew out of bounds.

FWEET! Coach Naranjo blew her whistle to stop play. "Kahn, your ball," she said. "Take it from the center, please."

"But it went out next to the goal," Nora said, turning to the coach. "I should get it at the corner."

"These are one-on-one rules," Coach replied. "And don't talk back, please."

Nora's face went slightly red as a teammate on the sidelines tossed her the ball. She stopped it with her chest and dribbled back to center.

This time, Nora charged with even more energy. Melina kept her eyes on the ball and tried to predict Nora's movements.

But Nora was too fast. She faked twice, whipped around Melina, then sprinted toward the goal.

Melina could hardly keep up. As she struggled to get in front of the goal, she stumbled over her own feet — and fell hard face-first into the grass.

Melina looked up just in time to see Nora score. The ball sailed into the top left corner. The shot was as perfect as the one Nora had made during the weave drill.

"Nice shot, Kahn!" Coach Naranjo called.

Melina pushed herself up, brushing off the grass and dirt from her uniform. She heard some of the girls snickering from the sidelines.

"It's your ball at the center, Stern," Coach instructed.

Melina nodded. She retrieved the ball from the goal and brought it to the center, her cheeks burning red with embarrassment and exhaustion. As soon as Coach blew her whistle, she took the ball under her toe.

Nora narrowed her eyes as Melina pulled the ball back and dribbled right. Melina quickly switched directions, but Nora kept with her.

Melina tried the through-the-legs trick, but Nora snapped her feet together. The ball rolled up

Nora's shin guards and she snatched possession. She darted around Melina and charged for another goal.

"Come on, Stern. Step it up!" It was Rose Torrence. The girls around her tried to hide their laughter.

Melina let out a frustrated breath. Jogging slowly down the field, she didn't even try to stop Nora. The ball sailed into the goal for another point.

Nora grabbed the ball from the goal and tossed it to Melina. "Two to nothing," she said, smiling.

"I know," Melina mumbled. She walked the ball to the center for another try.

"Two minutes left, girls," Coach Naranjo said.

Melina took control of the ball and dribbled wide right, keeping her eyes on the goal. Nora stuck with her, but this time Melina managed to slip around her with a spin. The goal was wide open.

"Shoot!" called Prissy. At least someone was rooting for Melina.

Melina pulled her leg back and shot — the ball went wide left.

"Wow," Nora said, coming up behind Melina. "Great shot, Stern," she added loudly, sounding as sarcastic as Rose Torrence.

"Um, are you serious?" said a voice from the sidelines. It was Torrence herself. "She got around *you*, didn't she?"

Rose's gang of friends laughed again, but now they were laughing at Nora.

It was Nora's ball. But as she drove toward the goal, Melina could tell a difference in her rival's moves. Her footwork was suddenly sloppy, and she seemed less sure of herself. Nora took a weak shot.

Melina easily blocked it and took control of the ball. She dribbled across the field, then took aim at the goal. It wasn't a great shot, either. But with no goalkeeper, it was good enough.

"Point for Stern!" Ms. Perez announced from the sidelines.

Prissy clapped for her, but Melina didn't feel like celebrating.

Before Nora could start another drive, Coach Naranjo blew her whistle. The one-on-one was over. Melina had lost, 2–1.

Coach clapped twice and called out to the team, "That's it for today. Please hustle to the locker rooms — the varsity team gets the field in five minutes."

Melina ran to pick up the ball. She passed by Rose and her friends. They were talking as they headed off the field.

"So much for saving the best for last," the captain muttered to the other girls.

Melina's face burned, but she ignored the older players. After she returned the ball to the mesh bag, she watched as the rest of the JV team filed into the locker room. But she couldn't bring herself to follow them.

She breathed hard and looked down at her shaky hands. Playing on JV was nothing like she'd hoped it would be.

CHAPTER 7

TRUCE

Instead of hurrying in to change with the rest of the team, Melina pulled on her sweats and hoodie. She climbed the aluminum bleachers and took a seat at the top. Soon the varsity girls jogged out onto the field.

Melina watched them stretch and warm up. They all seemed so much more grown-up and professional. The coach wasn't even on the field yet, but they were already starting to run drills.

"Looking good!" they called to one another. "Good hustle!" they cheered. "Great shot!" they shouted.

They move on the field like a well-oiled machine, Melina thought. *I wish I could be part of a team like that.*

"They're pretty good, huh?" It was Nora. She had slipped into the seat next to Melina while her attention was on the practice below.

"Yeah," Melina replied.

"That'll be me and you in a couple of years," Nora said.

Melina almost laughed. "If we survive the JV team."

"Yeah, that was pretty rough," Nora agreed, looking out over the field. Then she added quietly, "Sorry if I made it worse for you."

For a moment, Melina didn't say anything. "I don't even know if you did," she finally admitted. "I've just been really nervous since the tryouts.

The high schoolers kind of freaked me out. I didn't expect them to be such jerks. "

"Is that what was bothering you today?" Nora asked, surprised. "Jeez, I thought it was *me*."

"Well . . ." Melina started. She gave Nora a pointed look. "You haven't been exactly helping."

"Aww," said Nora, giving a little shove with her shoulder. "I mean, *I* was super nervous, but I didn't think you would be at all. I wouldn't have been acting like that if I had."

"You always act like that!" Melina exclaimed.

Nora looked confused. "Like what?" she asked.

"Like you want to beat me at everything!" Melina answered.

"Um, Mel?" Nora said. She gave one of her crooked grins. "That's how *you* act too."

Melina's face went hot. Not because she was mad, but because she was embarrassed. As she thought back to the surprise captain vote and all her sassy comebacks, Melina realized it was true. After all, it took two to create a rivalry. Nora hadn't done it on her own.

"Maybe I owe *you* an apology, then," Melina said.

Nora shook her head. "No . . . what I did today, trying to get the high schoolers to gang up on you, that was a low move," she said. "Rose and her friends don't need any encouragement! I just didn't want them giving *me* any problems. It was selfish. Sorry."

"Thanks. I get feeling scared, though. Rose and her friends are pretty intimidating," Melina said. She paused for a second. "Remember what a great duo we made on the middle school team last year?"

"Yeah, when Ms. Perez let us on the field," Nora added. "She always gave so much more game time to the eighth graders. And here we are, second string again."

Melina let her gaze drift back down to the field. She had known Nora a long time, probably as long as those varsity players down there had known each other. Maybe even longer.

"But we can still be a great duo," Melina said quietly. "We just have to put our rivalry aside."

Nora looked at Melina for a moment. A small smile tugged at the corner of her mouth. "You've got a deal," she said finally.

Nora put out her hand to shake on it, and Melina took it.

"So, no more competition between us?" Nora asked.

"For now, anyway," Melina said, grinning. "Now, we support each other."

"And we won't let Rose and her pals get to us?" Nora said.

Melina nodded, the nerves in her stomach finally disappearing. "Definitely not."

CHAPTER 8

BULLS VS. DRAGONS

The Bulloch High JV Bulls' first game was Saturday. Practice hadn't changed much throughout the week. The high school girls still treated the younger players like second-class teammates. Only now, Melina and Nora were working together better than ever.

"All right, ladies," Rose Torrence said, leaning into the pre-game huddle. "It's our first game, and we've had some rough practices."

Nora caught Melina's eye across the huddle with an excited grin. For the past week, Melina had seen Nora's smiles in a whole new way. It was almost hard to believe they were really friends. She had known Nora as nothing but a rival for so many years.

"But we've never lost an opening game to the Northend Dragons. We're not going to start now," Rose went on. Her eyes moved around the circle. She even offered a determined — if terrifying — smile to the three middle school girls.

"So on three, let's hear 'Go Bulls,' like you really mean it," Rose said. She put her hand in the middle of the circle. The rest of the team did the same. "One. Two. Three . . ."

"Go Bulls!" the girls shouted. They threw their hands up with the cheer to break up the huddle.

"This ought to be fun," Prissy said as she, Melina, and Nora walked to the bench.

At their second practice, Melina and Nora had been assigned to second-string forward positions, and Prissy was on second-string defense. It came as no surprise to any of them that the starting lineup was all ninth and tenth graders.

"Hey, we're still part of team," Melina reminded Prissy. "Even from the sidelines, we can support our teammates and keep it positive, right?"

Prissy gave a determined nod. "Right," she said.

The Northend Dragons, in green-and-yellow uniforms, jogged into position. The Bulls already stood on the field, ready to go.

The center referee called Rose and the other team captain for the coin toss. The Dragons captain called heads and won the flip. She high-fived the girls behind her as the ref placed the ball at center mark.

FWEET! The ref raised her arm and blew her whistle. The Dragons took the kick-off.

Melina leaned forward on the bench. Even if she wasn't on the field, she was still excited for the team's first game.

A Dragons striker knocked the ball forward into their captain's possession. She led her team on an attack up the right side.

The Bulls midfield played tight defense, but the Dragons center slipped through. When she passed to her right wing, though, the Bulls central defender — a tenth grader named Ivy — jumped forward.

Ivy pulled off a perfect steal and kicked the ball up the field to the Bulls' waiting strikers. Right away, Melina had to hand it to Rose Torrence. She was a skilled player.

Rose sprinted across the midfield, her right arm high to call out the play. She fired a perfect pass to Jana Brownstein.

Melina held her breath as Jana trapped the ball and got in place to shoot. The Dragons defenders were starting to rush her. Jana whipped back her leg and kicked.

But the Dragons goalkeeper dived just in time. She knocked it wide with both gloved hands.

Melina blew out a disappointed sigh. The other girls on the bench groaned at the miss.

"Good shot, Brownstein!" Rose called, applauding for her teammate. "Next time."

Melina looked at Nora and Prissy. Together, they jumped to their feet and started cheering.

"Way to go, Jana and Rose! Awesome effort!" Melina shouted from the sidelines.

It might not have been a goal, but it had still been a great play and a great shot. Soon the rest of the Bulls bench joined in, cheering for the starters.

As the bench quieted down, Melina nudged Prissy. "Who would've thought," she whispered, "that Rose Torrence would remind us to be positive?"

CHAPTER 9

GAME TIME

The score was tied 0–0. It was the second half, and none of the middle schoolers had been called in. But at the next throw-in, Coach Naranjo signaled for a substitution.

"Kahn, get in there," Ms. Perez called.

Nora jumped up from the bench. As soon as Jana crossed the sideline, she took the field.

"Go, Nora!" Melina shouted to her new friend.

"Great job, Jana," Prissy added to the older player as she walked over.

Jana didn't glance at Prissy or Melina. She hadn't

even slapped Nora's hand as they passed each other. She just stepped behind the bench and went straight for her water bottle.

Melina exchanged a glance with Prissy, then turned her attention back to the game. The Bulls were driving past the center line.

Nora was wide open down the field. Ivy kicked the ball toward her. But as it sailed over to Nora, Rose jumped in front of the ball. She trapped it with a chest bump and then went left.

"Wow, she just stole Nora's pass," Prissy muttered to Melina.

Nora caught their eyes from the pitch for an instant and then ran to the box to join the play. Rose took a shot on goal. It knocked the post and zoomed out of bounds.

"Good shot, Rose!" Jana yelled.

Melina and Prissy shared another glance, then clapped along with their teammate. But this time, they didn't feel it quite as much.

* * *

At the next throw-in, Ms. Perez waved in Melina and Prissy as Nora and Ivy left the field.

Melina's heart leapt into her throat as she took her spot on the pitch. She felt nervous and excited and terrified, but overall it was thrilling. This was her first time playing in a real JV game — a real *high* school soccer match.

But Melina quickly focused on the action on the field. She hovered at the center line as Prissy and the rest of the Bulls defense tried to clear the ball away from the goal.

When a Bulls defender rushed forward, the Dragons striker took a flimsy shot outside of the box. The keeper easily grabbed the ball and punted it high.

Melina ran with the ball, watching as it flew down the field. A girl in green got to it first. She kicked it back toward the Bulls goal.

But Rose stuck her foot out and trapped the ball. She started dribbling down field. Dodging around the Dragons defender, she passed to the open left winger, Kayla Thomas.

All three Bulls strikers moved into the box. Melina found herself open right off the post just as Kayla sent the ball across to Rose in the center.

"Torrence!" Melina called. "I'm open."

From the sidelines, she heard Nora and Prissy calling to Rose too.

"Get it to Stern!" Nora yelled.

"Look right, Torrence!" Prissy shouted.

Rose passed left instead, back to Kayla. Kayla shot, but the Dragons keeper was immediately on top of her. She easily snatched the ball and sent it back up field.

"Keep your eyes open, Torrence! You had open teammates," Coach Naranjo called out.

Rose gave a quick nod to the coach, but Melina saw her roll her eyes as they jogged from the goal.

Melina frowned. *Being a bad sport in practice is one thing,* she thought. *But if the high schoolers don't start playing like a team, we're going to lose this game!*

Before long, the Bulls defense got the ball back downfield. A midfielder headed it along the right sideline. Melina took the ball, then passed to Rose.

Rose dribbled strong up the middle as Kayla got open to her left. The three strikers moved into the box. Rose and Kayla were on the left, and Melina was on the right.

Rose drove to the goal. Kayla was tangled up with a defender, so Melina dropped back to the bottom corner of the box. The Dragons keeper was covering the left half of the goal as Rose approached.

"Behind you, Rose," Melina said. "I have the shot."

But Rose ignored her. She fired a line drive straight ahead — right into the keeper's arms. The Dragons keeper punted the ball high and long, clear across center line.

Melina blew out a frustrated sigh. They were still tied at 0–0, even though she had had two open shots on goal. If only Rose had given her the ball.

* * *

The game ended in a tie — neither team managed to get a goal, despite Coach Naranjo putting in all the starters for the final minutes of the game.

In the locker room, the team changed silently and was quickly filing out. No one seemed to be in the mood to stay and talk. But Melina hung back, sitting alone on the bench in front of her locker.

As Melina pulled off her shin guards, Coach Naranjo stuck her head into the locker room. "Rose, can I talk to you for a moment?" the coach asked.

"Sure thing, Coach," Rose replied, lifting her duffel bag onto her shoulder.

They went out of the room, but they must've stopped just outside of the door. Melina could still hear them talking.

"What were those missed two scoring opportunities about?" Coach Naranjo asked. "Why didn't you pass to Melina?"

"I swear I didn't see her, Coach," Rose insisted. "Both times I thought I had a good shot, so I took it."

Melina rolled her eyes at the captain's excuse. She didn't bother paying attention to the rest of their conversation. Instead, she thought about the game.

Melina wasn't disappointed they hadn't beaten their cross-town rivals. She wasn't even disappointed that she'd spent most of the game on the bench.

She was disappointed that the high schoolers weren't treating her like a teammate — on or off the field. Melina stared into her locker, thinking about what she would do if she were the team captain.

After a moment of thought, she set her mind to it and changed out of her uniform. A determined smile spread across her lips.

Just because I'm not the captain doesn't mean I can't start acting like one, she told herself. *At least a little bit.*

CHAPTER 10

VICE CAPTAIN

When Melina walked into Delano Middle School on Monday morning, Nora and Prissy were already waiting for her at her locker.

"Mel," Prissy said. "We have to talk."

"About what?" Melina asked.

"About what?" Nora repeated. "Were you at the same game I was on Saturday? You had an open goal. Twice!"

Melina nodded as she put her coat away. "I know. If I were the team captain, I'd tell those tenth graders a few things about playing as a team."

Prissy sighed. "Too bad you're *not* captain," she said. "I'd prefer you over Rose Torrence any day."

"Well, captain or not," Melina said, "I've been thinking about it all weekend."

"Wait, are you going to say something to Rose and her crew?" Nora asked eagerly.

Melina didn't say anything. She just grinned.

"Ooh, you are!" Prissy exclaimed, clasping her hands together. "Can I be there?"

"Me too!" Nora said with a bright smile.

"I'm not looking for drama," Melina said. "I just want to remind her we're all on the same team."

"Aw, fine," Nora said as the two-minute warning buzzer sounded. "But after, I want to hear all about it."

* * *

Melina hurried from their last-hour class. Nora caught her eye as she flew out the door and flashed a thumbs-up and encouraging grin. Melina skipped the stop at her locker and went straight across the athletic field to the Bulloch Bulls locker rooms.

She scooted past Coach Naranjo's office, waving as she passed. The coach hardly looked up. She just threw up one hand to acknowledge Melina.

But Melina didn't mind. She wasn't there to see the coach. She was there to see the captain.

Stopping just outside of the locker room, Melina took a deep breath. Then she pushed the door open.

She found Rose Torrence standing by the first row of lockers. Jana and Kayla were with her. They sat on a bench, laughing as Rose cracked jokes.

Melina strode right up to them. "Hi," she said.

"What do you want?" the captain asked.

Melina sat down next to Kayla. "Too bad we couldn't pull out the win on Saturday, huh?" she said, glancing at each of the girls.

"Yeah, too bad," Rose said, dropping her eyes to the ground. Her face went red. Melina couldn't tell if she was embarrassed or angry. Maybe both.

"The tenth-grade girls play a tight game," Melina went on. "Your teamwork is really solid."

"Thanks," Kayla said, shifting on the bench.

"Wait a minute," Rose said, dropping onto the bench between Kayla and Melina. "Are you *admitting* that we lost because of you middle school girls?"

Melina smiled. "I wouldn't say that," she said. "I'm more saying half the work is done. The other half will be getting you high school girls to work better with us middle school girls."

"What's that supposed to mean?" Jana asked.

"It means that our team might be great," Melina said, standing up to face all three girls on the bench. "But right now, it's not."

"Yeah," Rose huffed, "because you middle schoolers came along and dropped the skill curve."

"Or," Melina countered, "it's because you haven't accepted us as members of the team."

"Of course we haven't," Rose said with a sneer. "Would you in our place?"

Melina shrugged. "I'm not sure. I haven't been in your place. But to be honest, sometimes last year I'd look at the sixth grade girls and wish they could pick it up a little, you know?"

Kayla laughed, but Rose elbowed her in the ribs.

"But that doesn't mean I didn't pass to them during games," Melina continued. "It doesn't mean I treated them badly or made them feel unwanted. Because no matter what, they were still my teammates."

Rose didn't say anything. Jana sniffed and kicked her toe against the open locker door in front of her. "Whatever," she mumbled.

"She's right," said Coach Naranjo as she stepped into view from around the corner. "And I'm as guilty as you three have been."

"Oh, Coach, I didn't mean —" Melina said, but the coach cut her off with a wave of her hand.

"No, you didn't," Coach said, "but I've been letting the ninth and tenth graders get away with a lot of rude behavior. Not only is it unfair to you and the other middle schoolers, but it cost us the game on Saturday. That's not how I want to run my team."

She looked at the high school girls. "I will not be allowing any more childish behavior. You're all on the same team. I expect you to act like it. Now, get out to the pitch and start running laps."

Rose and her friends hopped to it. Melina stood alone with Coach Naranjo.

"Coach," Melina started, "I haven't had a chance to tell you yet, but I'm a big fan of yours."

"Yeah?" Coach said.

Melina nodded. "I saw you play for the varsity team when I was seven," she said. "I've wanted to play for the varsity Bulls ever since."

"I'm flattered. Thanks, Melina," Coach Naranjo replied. "And I've been thinking. You're right — the middle school girls aren't really feeling like part of the team yet."

"What should we do about it?" Melina asked. "I can talk to the girls from Delano."

"I'm sure you will," Coach Naranjo said, smiling, "which is how I know I've made the right choice for vice captain."

Melina squinted at the coach. "What's that?" she asked. "Is that a thing?"

"It is now," Coach Naranjo answered. "Look, Rose is captain because she's tough, loud, and can really perform on the pitch. But that doesn't mean she couldn't use a little help from you."

"Me?" Melina said.

"It's only fair," the coach said with a shrug. "The middle school team voted for you. Who am I to question election results?"

Melina laughed. "I guess you're right."

"Of course I'm right," said Coach Naranjo. "I'm the coach!"

CHAPTER 11

ONE FOR ALL

The next week of JV practices were the best yet. With Melina as the new vice captain, the middle school girls finally felt like part of the team. And after Melina's talk and Coach's official support, even Rose had grudgingly accepted them as full members.

Saturday morning was the Bulls' next game. This time they were facing up against the Old Town Owls. Rose and Melina stood side-by-side in the team huddle.

"All right, on three," Rose said. She *was* the loud one, after all. "All for one, one for all. One, two, three!"

"All for one!" the team shouted together. "One for all!"

As the JV Bulls got into position, Melina, Nora, and Prissy headed to the bench. They weren't starting again, but it was okay. Melina knew they weren't the strongest players on the team — vice captain or not.

For the first half of the game, both teams were scoreless. Melina hoped she would get some playtime, but the high school girls were fired up and playing hard. Even though no subs were called for, the three middle schoolers still cheered wildly at every opportunity.

The Bulls took the kickoff to start the second half. The first drive was strong, and Rose set up Jana for a clear shot on goal. But the Owls keeper was quick. She grabbed the ball and punted it clear.

Both teams were playing aggressively. The Owls charged on the Bulls goal. Their center faked left, sending the Bulls keeper in a dive the wrong way. The Owls player fired a shot into the right corner.

Melina and the whole bench gasped as the ball just caught the outside of the post and flew out of bounds. It was the Bulls' ball.

With only a few minutes left on the play clock, Rose and Jana attacked. Rose put her foot on top of the ball and pulled it back, then charged down the side. She passed across the box.

"Come on, Bulls!" Melina yelled, jumping off the bench.

Jana took the ball and broke away from her defender after some smooth footwork. She sprinted forward, then launched a strong shot.

The Owls keeper dove. The ball hit her gloves and rolled off to the side, crossing the thick white line next to the goal. The Bulls had a corner kick.

But something was wrong. Jana wasn't getting ready for the kick — she was lying on the field, clutching her thigh.

Melina watched with worry as the ref and Coach Naranjo jogged over to the injured player. "Did you see what happened?" Melina asked the other middle schoolers.

Nora and Prissy shook their heads. "But she must've strained her hamstring," Nora said. "When she was sprinting toward the goal or when she made the shot."

Slowly, Jana got to her feet with Coach's help. Melina and the rest of the team clapped for Jana as she came off the field, limping.

"That was a great shot, Jana," Melina said.

Jana grimaced as she sat down on the bench, but she gave Melina a tight smile. "Thanks. It looks like you'll be finishing the game now — go get 'em for me."

Melina gave a determined nod. "Will do."

Sure enough, Coach Naranjo waved her over. "Stern, you're in for Jana. Kahn and Wilkins," she called, "you're up too. Let's see if we can switch things up a bit."

Melina and the two girls ran onto the field as two other Bulls players came off the field. She and Nora went in as forwards. Prissy took her place on defense.

Rose slammed the corner kick to where Melina, Nora, and two other Bulls were grouped in front of the goal, just inside the box. Melina jumped for the header, but an Owls defender jumped higher. The girl headed the ball back. Another Owls player swooped in and sent it flying down the field.

Luckily, Prissy and the defense were ready. Ivy cut off the striker at the box and stole the ball. She passed to Prissy, who launched the ball past midfield.

Rose was there, ready to take control. The captain dribbled through the Owls backfield, and then passed to Nora, who had gotten free along the left sideline.

Melina and Rose closed in together on the box. The Owls defenders ran into place, ready to protect their goal.

Heading toward the box, Nora dribbled down the left. She spun twice to lose her defenders. The goalkeeper moved close to the left post, making sure Nora couldn't get an open shot.

"Loosen up!" Nora called to Rose and Melina in the box.

Rose dropped back to the top of the box. Melina swept across to the right side, where the goal was wide open. The three strikers were working perfectly together.

With only seconds left, Nora drew back like she was going to take the shot, but then she hit the ball with the inside of her foot. The ball sailed to Rose at the top of the box. Rose started to drive on goal, before quickly passing to Melina.

Melina took possession. The goal was wide open. She could almost take her time as she launched the ball into the right side of the net.

GOAL!

"Yes!" Melina shouted, pumping her fist.

Nora was the first one to throw an arm around her. "Great shot, Mel!" she exclaimed.

Prissy met her at center line and grabbed her for a hug. "One nothing!" she cried. "Nice shot."

As the ref blew the whistle to signal the end of the game, Rose nudged Melina. "Pretty good shot," she said.

"Thanks for the pass," Melina replied as they walked together to shake hands with the Owls. "See? We make a pretty good team after all."

Rose smiled. "You got it, vice captain."

ABOUT the AUTHOR

Eric Stevens lives in St. Paul, Minnesota. He is studying to become a middle school English teacher. Eric has written numerous books for the Jake Maddox Girl Sports Stories, Jake Maddox Sports Stories, and Jake Maddox JV series. Some of his favorite things include pizza, playing video games, watching cooking shows on TV, riding his bike, and trying new restaurants. Some of his least favorite things include olives and shoveling snow.

GLOSSARY

drill (DRIL) – a repetitive exercise that helps you learn a specific skill

exhausting (ig-ZAWST-ing) – extremely tiring

glared (GLAIRD) – looked at in an angry and threatening way

impromptu (im-PROMP-too) – not planned ahead of time

pitch (PICH) – a chiefly British term for a field of play; often used by American soccer players

relieved (ri-LEEVD) – feeling happy and relaxed because something difficult or unpleasant has gone away or been made easier

rival (RYE-vuhl) – a person who is trying to achieve the same goal or trying to be better than someone else; a competitor

roster (ROSS-tur) – a list of players on a team

scrimmage (SKRIM-ij) – a practice game

second string (SEK-uhnd STRING) – players available to replace those who start the game

DISCUSSION QUESTIONS

1. Melina wasn't very confident during her first JV practice, and she struggled to play well. Using examples from the story, discuss some possible reasons why she was having trouble.

2. Talk about why Melina and Nora decided to set aside their rivalry. How did it help them? Be sure to support your answer with examples from the story.

3. Melina's feelings about the JV team changed a lot throughout the book. Talk about how she felt before tryouts, then talk about how she felt after tryouts. What caused the change? Use examples from the story to support your answer.

WRITING PROMPTS

1. Look back through the text and find four descriptions of Nora's smile. What do they tell you about Nora's character? Do the descriptions of her smile ever change? Write a paragraph about it.

2. Melina decided to stand up to Rose and her friends. Write two paragraphs about a time you decided to stand up for yourself or for someone else. Be sure to explain why you did it and what happened afterward.

3. A theme, or main idea, in this story is that a team needs to work together and respect each other to be successful. Write a list of things you could do to encourage teamwork. In your list, include ways that Melina and the other characters built up their team, but also come up with some of your own.

MORE ABOUT SOCCER

The first **FIFA Women's World Cup** was held in 1991. The United States team beat Norway 2–1 in the final game. This was 61 years after the first *men's* World Cup.

The Women's World Cup is held every four years. As of 2016, only four countries have won the championship. The **United States** has taken first place three times, **Germany** has won twice, and **Japan** and **Norway** have each won once.

Cleats date back all the way to 1526! Because the studs on the bottom of the shoe grip into the ground, cleats help a player make quick turns, stops, and starts, as well as prevent slipping.

The classic black-and-white **soccer ball** was first introduced by Adidas at the 1970 Men's World Cup. It's made of twenty white hexagons and twelve black pentagons.

There are often three **forwards** on a team. Forwards play closest to the opponent's goal and are the most likely to score. A forward can also be called a **striker**, but sometimes the term is used to refer to the forward that is the primary scorer.

U.S. forward and 2012 FIFA Player of the Year **Abby Wambach** currently holds the record for most goals scored in international games — in either men's or women's soccer. In 252 international games, she scored **184 times** (77 of the shots were headers!).

American player **Hope Solo** is one of the top goalkeepers in women's soccer history. Solo helped the U.S. team win two Olympic gold medals in 2008 and 2012, and she's received the **Golden Glove** award for best goalkeeping in both the 2011 and 2015 FIFA Women's World Cups. She also holds a number of professional records, including shutouts, wins, starts, and longest undefeated streak.

Corner kicks are awarded when a defender sends the ball over the end line by her own goal. Corner kicks are considered good scoring opportunities.

In 1987, soccer star **Mia Hamm** joined the **United States Women's National Team** when she was only fifteen years old, making her the youngest player ever on the team.